Friends Have Fun

Metro Early Reading Program

Level A, Stories 6–10

Credits
Illustration: Front cover, Lane Gregory
Photography: Front and back covers, Mark Segal/Tony Stone Images

ISBN 1-58120-645-3

2 3 4 5 6 7 8 9 CL 03 02 01 00

Table of Contents

Did you see Jed?
His sand castle is
so good.
He did not have a kit.
All he had was a mug
and a pot.

3

5

7

9

10

11

12

I see what that dog did.
But he is not my dog!

15

16

Story 7

19

20

21

25

There is the rap of the nut.
There is the buzz of
the bugs.
There is the pat of the cat.
There is the yap of the dog.
What can I do?

28

30

31

The squirrel did get the nut.
I let the bugs out of the net.
The dog and cat can nap.
And then I can have a good
long nap.

Story 8

34

After that, can we see the rabbit? I see one on the map.

35

38

That rabbit
can hop.
We can not
have a rabbit
for a pet.
We do not
have a pen.

39

41

The men have
good zoo hats.
Tasha, you can
get a fox hat
or a rabbit hat.
You can get
this hen hat
from the men.

43

44

45

47

Story 9

50

52

There are no pig wigs.
But we can work on
a pig jig.

54

55

Chapter 1: We Play

Can we go to the zoo?

66

No, Tasha.
We have to go to work
with Mom.
But it will not be so bad.
We can have a good day.

67

73

75

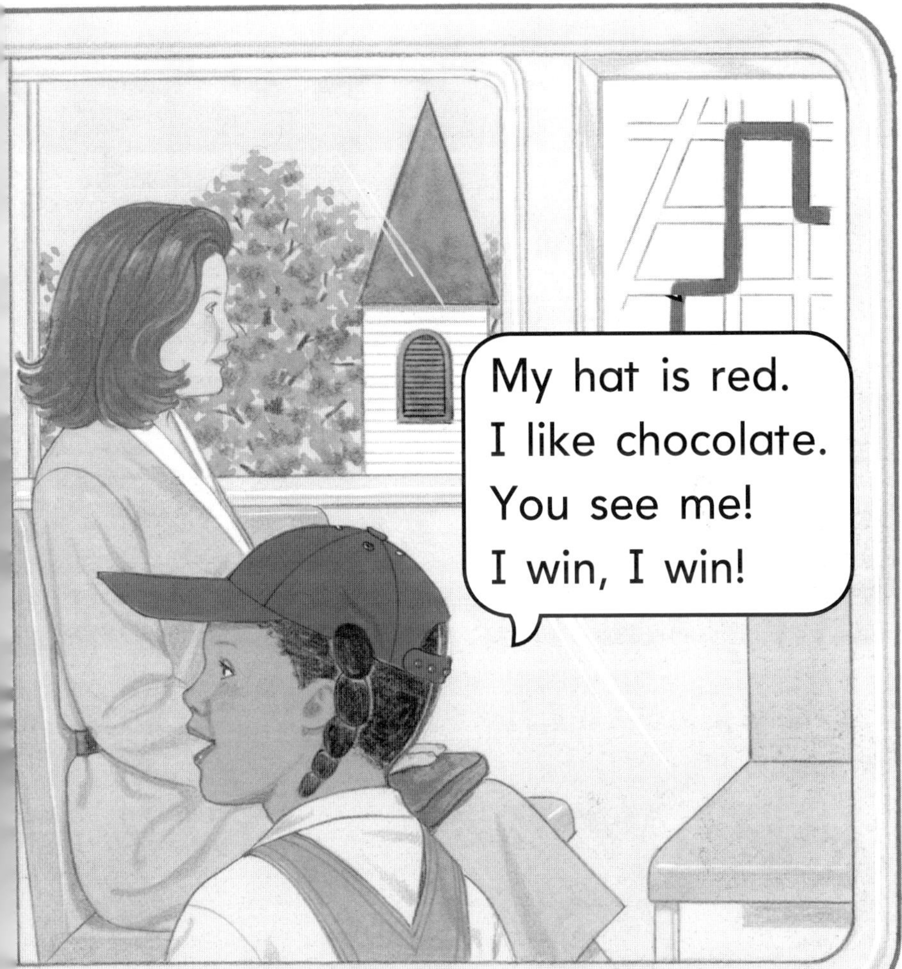
My hat is red.
I like chocolate.
You see me!
I win, I win!

I do not like work.
I like to go to the zoo.
Can we go to the zoo?

88

We have a new rabbit.
This will be his pen.
Can you mop it out, Ben?
Here is a mop.

90

93

Skills and Vocabulary

Story 6: Get Rid of That Dog

First Review

initial consonants:
d, k

New

phonograms:
-id, -og

decodable words:
dog, dug, kid, kit, rid

sight words:
come, here, his, if, make, our

story words:
castle, sand

Skills and Vocabulary

Story 7: No! Not Again!

First Review

initial consonants:
n, y

New

phonograms:
-ap, -ut

decodable words:
nap, net, nut, rap, yap

sight words:
again, cat, then, there, this

story words:
buzz, squirrel

Story 8: At the Zoo

First Review

initial consonant:
z

New

phonograms:
-en, -op

decodable words:
den, fox, hen, hop, map, men, mop, pen

sight words:
after, has, how, new, or

story words:
rabbit, zoo

Skills and Vocabulary

Story 9: Three Pigs and a Wolf

First Review

initial consonants:
j, w

New

phonograms:
-ig, -in

decodable words:
big, jig, pig, wig, win

sight words:
are, give, three, us, work

story words:
play, wolf

Story 10: A Day with Mom

Review Story

No new phonics elements or sight words.